Beyond
BOUNDARIES

KAUSTAV M KASHYAP

BLUEROSE PUBLISHERS
India | U.K.

Copyright © Kaustav M Kashyap 2025

All rights reserved by author. No part of this publication may be reproduced, stored in a retrieval system or transmitted in any form or by any means, electronic, mechanical, photocopying, recording or otherwise, without the prior permission of the author. Although every precaution has been taken to verify the accuracy of the information contained herein, the publisher assume no responsibility for any errors or omissions. No liability is assumed for damages that may result from the use of information contained within.

BlueRose Publishers takes no responsibility for any damages, losses, or liabilities that may arise from the use or misuse of the information, products, or services provided in this publication.

For permissions requests or inquiries regarding this publication, please contact:

BLUEROSE PUBLISHERS
www.BlueRoseONE.com
info@bluerosepublishers.com
+91 8882 898 898
+4407342408967

ISBN: 978-93-7018-277-6

Cover design: Daksh
Typesetting: Tanya Raj Upadhyay

First Edition: April 2025

PROLOUGE

Beneath the vast skies where history etches the tales of great wars—fought for power, land, and the illusion of permanence—there lies another battlefield, silent and marked not by the banners or blood, but by the turmoil of the human souls. Can there be a battlefield where no armies clash, no cannons roar, and no victors are crowned ?? Instead, a solitary war waged within, where the adversaries are fear, doubt, comfort, privilege, and prejudice !! Are these wars unrecorded in the annals of history, are less profound?? The victor of such wars may not be glorified with statues or songs, but they carry the quiet strength of transformation with the delicate scars of growth. They shape the spirit in ways the world may never notice.

In such silent war, fear looms like an unyielding shadow, doubt whispers of failure, and comfort lulls the soul into complacency, privilege and prejudice binds. Yet, in the heart of this struggle lies the possibility of light—a chance to break free, to rise above, and to become something truer, braver, and more of a whole.

A shiver ran through Arya's being, as if the echo of a distant battle kindled within him, whispering the turmoil of a war waged in silence.

As the Biggest Temple of the village brimmed with joy and devotion, the smell of incense hung heavy in the air, curling upward like silent whispers. Men in crisp white dhotis, women with traditional attire moved with practiced grace, their movements devout, their voices murmuring prayers that had echoed through generations. The sacred altar stood at the centre, adorned with marigold garlands and shimmering lamps, a stage set for the Puja ritual that would soon begin. Arya watched from a distance, his heart caught in a strange dissonance of longing and unease. Just a year ago, he would have stood among the chosen, his presence called upon to perform the rituals that carried the weight of tradition. A privileged heir to his family's lineage, he had once been a fixture in such ceremonies—a symbol of honour and continuity.

But now, he stood apart. Uninvited.

The exclusion was not a spoken decree but a deliberate silence, one that shouted louder than any words. The priests' eyes slid past him as though he no longer existed. The crowd, too, seemed to shift subtly, their gazes laced with questions they dared not voice aloud. Arya felt their judgment like a weight pressing against his chest. Their eyes seemed to say. *He no longer belongs.* He clenched his fists at his sides, the fabric of his kurta bunching beneath his fingers. The ache in his chest was not just one of anger or sadness but of something deeper—fear. It was a quiet, insidious fear, one that had crept into his life as he began to question the very traditions that had shaped him.

The fear of losing privilege had been his first reckoning. It struck like a blow the moment he realized that his dissent came at a price. No longer was he the favoured son of the community, loved and celebrated . The rituals, the respect, the subtle deference of others—these had vanished as swiftly as they had come.

He remembered the first time he had voiced his unease about the hierarchies embedded in their traditions. Arya had already felt the shift within himself, a fracture in the foundation of the world he had once accepted without question. The privilege he had enjoyed began to feel hollow, a gilded cage that chained him to traditions he no longer believed in. And now, as he stood on the temple's edge, cast out from the centre of the very world he was born into, that cage had crumbled completely.

Behind the fear of losing privilege, there loomed deeper fears—of abandonment, of disappointing his family, of becoming an outcast in both his community and his home. What if his father never forgive him? What if his mother's gentle smile turned into a pained silence? What if his sisters, other relatives, once his closest confidants, could no longer look him in the eye?

These fears weighed on him like lead, pulling him in two directions. One path led back to the safety of conformity, privilege, honour and roles that had defined him for so long. The other path—the one his heart yearned for—was shrouded in uncertainty, a lonely road where his only guide was the quiet voice of his conscience. He wanted to ignore that voice. He wanted to believe that the world would not judge him so harshly if he simply stayed silent. But the voice would not let him rest. It whispered to him in the quiet hours of the night, the questions he could no longer ignore. The crowd began to move, forming a half-circle around the altar as the priests prepared to begin. Arya lingered in the shadows, unsure if he should stay or leave. His absence would be noticed, just as surely as his presence was ignored.

Arya paused for a moment.

As he walked away from the temple, Arya knew his path would not be easy. He would have to face his family's disappointment, the community's disdain, and the sharp loneliness of being misunderstood. Fear would accompany him every step of the way, whispering its doubts and insecurities. But for the first time, Arya felt something stronger than fear. A spark of purpose, small but steady, burned within him. He did not yet know where it would lead, but he knew he could no longer turn back.

And so, Arya walked into the unknown, carrying with him the weight of his fears—and the courage to face them.

Table of Contents

Chapter 0 Inception of the Battleground...................... 1

Chapter I Sunshine before a storm 9

Chapter II The Heart's Rebellion................... 16

Chapter III The Silent Chains of Tradition and First Signs of Disapproval 24

Chapter IV War Within and The Reflection of Dharma 32

Chapter V Facing-off the Battlefield............................ 40

Chapter VI Crossing the Threshold 48

Chapter VII The True Victory..................................... 54

Chapter 0
Inception of the Battleground

In a society shaped by age-old customs and the rigid lines of caste, where Brahmins are ranked in the highest, Arya, a thirty-seven-year-old Brahmin, wise beyond his age, found himself embroiled in a battle no one could see. Raised in a world carved by tradition and bounded by the high walls of caste, he carried the legacy of his ancestors within him—a legacy that both defined and confined him. Arya, a man of books and introspection, held his lineage with reverence and pride, a pride that sometimes conflicted with the deeper truths that lay dormant within him.

Arya had grown up steeped in the values of his family, inheriting a rich tapestry of customs and beliefs. He was taught to honour the line of ancestors from which he came and to carry their values into the future. His family cherished their heritage and customs, and the age-old honour of his caste was a fundamental part of his identity. For Arya, his lineage was more than a family tree—it was a foundation built upon reverence for the past, pride in the present, and responsibility for the future.

Yet, life has a way of shifting one's understanding, particularly when one stands at the crossroads of love and tradition. Arya's world was not one of simplicity; it was a complex web where dignity was often mistaken for privilege, and tradition was worshipped, sometimes blindly. He had come to see that love and dignity transcended birth and station, that love was pure, and dignity was a right—not a privilege. In his understanding, love should not be bound by the rigid walls of social status or background. Everyone, he believed, should have the right to love, be loved and to be treated with respect, no matter where they came from or who they were born to be.

In a quiet, unremarkable corner of his life, Arya met her. She entered his world in the most ordinary of ways, but there was nothing ordinary about her. She was a woman who carried within her both the fragility and strength of someone who had survived society's scorn—a divorced woman from a caste deemed "lower," a mother to a young girl with eyes wide and bright as though daring the world to judge her, to look down upon her mother who stood, defiant and unapologetic. In her, Arya saw no stigma, no blemish on his honour. Instead, he saw resilience, purity, and a love untainted by caste—a spirit of unadulterated dignity that no tradition could define.

The woman Arya loved was anything but diminished by these judgments. She stood tall, embodying a quiet resilience that defied the narrow confines of her society's expectations. Her struggles had etched lines of wisdom on her face, but her eyes still held a fire that refused to be extinguished. As a single mother, she had carried the weight of her child's future on her shoulders, navigating a world that sought to diminish her worth with every step. Yet, she walked forward with unwavering determination, her dignity intact and her spirit unbroken. Her kindness remained untainted by the bitterness of rejection, and her laughter was a testament to her courage, ringing out as an act of rebellion against the silence the community demanded.

As a teacher by profession, she carried herself with unwavering dedication, pouring her heart into nurturing young minds despite the shadows of prejudice that loomed over her. Each day, she stepped into the classroom with a renewed sense of purpose, treating her profession not just as a job but as a calling. To Arya, she was not a woman stained by shame but a symbol of strength—an embodiment of the grace it took to live unapologetically against the tide of prejudice.

To Arya, she embodied something pure, something uncontaminated by society's prejudices. In her, he found not dishonour but a love unbreakable and true. She was a gift, one he felt bound to protect, though he knew he was now stepping into a war his family would never approve. To them, she was an outsider, a disturbance in the ancient order, a threat to the sanctity they had guarded for generations. This woman was everything his family would never have chosen for him. And so, Arya stood at a crossroad , torn between two truths, two paths. His conscience whispered one truth, yet his lineage demanded another. The battleground had been set within his soul, an inner war between love and tradition, between the new world he yearned to embrace and the old one that had shaped him.

For Arya, this was not a fight he had ever anticipated. Life had taught him that battles were fought outside, in the fields, in the courts, or in politics. He had never imagined that the fiercest battle would unfold within him, that his greatest opponent would be his own loyalty to the past, to his family, to the values he had cherished. But love has a way of turning certainties into questions, of taking the strongest foundations and shaking them to their core.

He found himself asking: What does honour mean? Is it to uphold the traditions set by others, or is it to live by the truth he knew in his heart? And if he chose love, would that choice make him a lesser man? Arya was not a man who took his promises lightly; his word was his bond, his honour unyielding. But love, he recognised, had a way of slipping past the walls built around one's soul, erasing boundaries that once seemed unbreakable.

The woman he loved did not come from his world, and yet, she had shown him a world he had never known—a world where love was pure, where dignity did not depend on caste or status, and where courage was defined by defying societal scorn. She had lived a life that, to many, would seem a mark of shame. But to Arya, her past was not a blemish; it was a badge of resilience, a testament to her strength, and a mirror to his own soul's unspoken desires.

As he looked into her eyes, he found an answer he did not want to accept. This woman was not just a choice; she was his truth, the part of him that society could never understand. In her presence, he felt a freedom that he had never known before, a release from the shackles of expectation that had bound him since birth.

But to embrace her would be to renounce the life he had known. It would mean defying the elders who had watched over him, stepping outside the lineage that had given him his identity, and relinquishing the honour that had been his family's pride. His conscience wrestled with the implications, while his heart whispered a quiet truth: love, when it is real, cannot be constrained by tradition or defined by the rules set by others.

In the end, Arya's love was not just for a woman—it was a love that yearned for freedom, for the right to live authentically. And yet, the path he yearned to walk was strewn with thorns. Each step brought him closer to a life of conflict, a world where his every action would be judged, where his name would no longer evoke pride but whispers of rebellion. He knew his family would see him not as a man in love but as a son who had chosen disgrace over duty.

Still, Arya could not turn away. He had glimpsed a truth greater than his family's expectations, and that truth compelled him to fight. It was not an easy battle; it was a war that would be fought in every glance, every word, and every breath. His resolve was tested by each disapproving look, every quiet conversation that seemed to carry his family's dismay. And with every protest, Arya felt the weight of centuries bearing down on him—the traditions that had bound his forefathers, the legacy that defined his family's name, and the whispers of duty that echoed through the halls of his childhood home.

Arya knew that his choice would not just affect him; it would ripple through his entire family, shaking the foundation upon which they had built their lives. He would no longer be just Arya, the dutiful son; he would become a symbol of defiance, a man who dared to love in a world that had no place for such love.

And so, Arya found himself at the dawn of a holy war, a war that would be fought not with swords or words but with the quiet strength of his heart. This was the battle for his soul, a fight to live not as a son bound by duty, but as a man bound by love. In this battleground of the heart, every glance, every silent prayer, and every decision would be a testament to the strength of his conviction. He stood on the brink of a choice that would define him—not as a man of tradition, but as a man of truth.

As he prepared to face his family, Arya understood that the path he was about to walk was one that would leave scars. But he also knew that some scars were worth bearing. For in this war, fought within the depths of his soul, lay the promise of a life unbound, a life where love was not dictated by birth or blood but by the quiet strength of two hearts that dared to defy the world.

The battleground was set, and Arya stood ready. In this holy war, he was both warrior and witness, both bound and free, a man torn between love and tradition, yet guided by a truth that even centuries of custom could not silence.

Chapter I
Sunshine before a storm

Arya's life was a well-orchestrated symphony, a melody that played seamlessly through the phases of his youth. Born into a respected Brahmin family known for its adherence to traditional values and principles, Arya was surrounded by the warmth and structure of a large family, having two loving sisters, uncles-aunts and a branch of caring cousins. His father, a Professor by profession, man of high regard in their community, provided a solid foundation, one built upon the tenets of education, respect, and responsibility. Arya's mother, a teacher by profession, gentle yet steadfast, embodied the grace and resilience that shaped Arya's sense of duty and compassion. Together, they raised Arya in an environment of support and encouragement, giving him both roots and wings.

Arya excelled academically from an early age, a trait much admired in his family and society. The family celebrated his every achievement, small or large, with pride and joy. His relatives often remarked on how Arya's hard work and dedication were reflections of his father's discipline and his mother's unwavering commitment. But beyond the admiration lay a certain expectation – Arya was the family's torchbearer, the one expected to make everyone proud.

His journey in academia reached new heights when he secured a place in a reputed institution for a degree in Petroleum Engineering. Here, Arya blossomed in more ways than one. Living away from home for the first time, he embraced the freedom of hostel life, relishing in the late-night study sessions, the camaraderie among friends, and the thrill of living independently. His academic performance was stellar; Arya graduated with a first-class degree, making his family and himself proud. It was a triumph that not only affirmed his hard work but also set the tone for the future that awaited him.

With an eye toward growth, Arya then moved to a prestigious university outside his state to pursue a Master's degree in Oil & Gas Management. Nestled in a picturesque hill city, the university was a place of new beginnings, beautiful landscapes, and friendships that Arya would carry with him for years. The quiet hills and majestic mountains seemed to resonate with Arya's young and thoughtful nature. Here, he found himself once again surrounded by like-minded individuals who shared his aspirations and ambitions, and he relished the intellectual stimulation and friendship. Arya continued to excel, earning a first-class degree and adding another feather to his cap. He was on a well-defined path, one that many young professionals in his field aspired to follow.

Upon completing his studies, Arya joined a prominent Oil Company. His first role was challenging yet fulfilling, and he threw himself into his work with the same passion and determination that had driven him throughout his academic journey. The early days of his career were exhilarating, marked by new responsibilities, teamwork, and a sense of accomplishment. The oil industry offered him everything he had dreamed of – a lucrative career, intellectual challenges, and the potential for rapid advancement. He was often accredited for his diligence and innovative approach, and it didn't take long before Arya began to envision a future on the international stage.

With his track record, the prospect of a career abroad seemed not just possible but probable. Arya's eyes were set on this horizon, on the opportunity to work in global oil markets and immerse himself in diverse cultures. He knew that moving abroad would open doors to cutting-edge technology, professional growth, and significant financial rewards. His friends, too, encouraged him to take the plunge, convinced that Arya's ambition and abilities would lead him to success.

But fate, as it often does, had other plans. One evening, after a long day at work, Arya found himself alone with his thoughts. He reflected on his career, his goals, and the journey he had taken so far. He thought of his parents back home, who were now growing older. Their strength, which had once seemed unshakable, was now touched with traces of age. Arya felt a pull in his heart, a quiet but powerful call that asked him to consider a different path. Could he leave his parents at a time when they needed him the most? Could he pursue personal success when his family, his roots, awaited his presence?

It was a moment of profound introspection, one that altered the trajectory of Arya's life. In the days that followed, he made the decision to return home, not out of obligation but out of love and a sense of responsibility. The decision was met with mixed reactions. His parents, initially surprised, expressed concerns about the shift in his plans. After all, Arya had a promising career ahead of him, one that offered both stability and prestige. Why would he want to leave all that behind?

But Arya's conviction was unwavering. He told his parents, with sincerity that he wanted to be closer to them-not only out of duty but out of love. He longed to be a part of their everyday moments, to hold place in their lives, just as they had lovingly done for him all along. It was a sentiment they couldn't refuse, even if they hesitated to fully understand it. Gradually, they came to see Arya's decision not as a step back but as a choice rooted in deep family values and love.

Back in his hometown, Arya faced a new challenge – the pursuit of entrepreneurship. He had the education, the skills, and a keen understanding of the oil and gas industry. But starting a company from the ground up was uncharted territory. Determined to make it work, Arya channelled his energy and focus into building his own business. He envisioned a venture that would not only benefit him personally but also contribute to his community. It was a challenging period filled with late nights, strategic planning, and countless meetings. But Arya thrived under pressure, his dedication becoming the cornerstone of his entrepreneurial journey.

Though his parents were initially uncertain, they slowly became his biggest supporters. They saw the sincerity in Arya's efforts, his drive to create something meaningful, and his commitment to the family. His friends, too, rallied around him, offering both encouragement and practical advice. They admired Arya's courage to walk away from a conventional path to create something of his own. Arya's reputation as an "ideal son" in the eyes of his relatives and community only grew. Here was a man who had not only achieved academic and professional success but had also chosen a path aligned with his values and responsibilities.

In the months that followed, Arya's company began to take shape. His hard work, combined with his knowledge and passion, paid off as he established a steady footing in the industry. He quickly gained a reputation for integrity and innovation, drawing the respect of his peers and the admiration of his community. His decision to stay close to home and pursue entrepreneurship resonated with many, earning him the love and support of everyone around him. Arya had successfully bridged the gap between ambition and duty, balancing his professional aspirations with his personal values.

As he navigated the challenges of running a business, Arya found himself feeling more fulfilled than ever. Each success, each milestone, was shared with his family, friends, and community, making the journey all the more rewarding. His life had indeed taken an unexpected turn, one that had once seemed daunting but had since become a source of immense pride and joy.

For Arya, life continued to unfold in a series of perfect tunes, each note resonating with purpose and harmony. He had found a balance between the demands of the world and the love of his family, between personal success and communal values. He was not just an ideal son but an example for his community, a man who had shown that sometimes, the most fulfilling path is the one that brings us back home.

Chapter II
The Heart's Rebellion

Despite Arya's unwavering dedication to his family, an uncontainable love stirred within him, a force powerful enough to breach the boundaries of his disciplined soul. This love was unlike any he had ever known. It was a quiet storm, a longing he could neither deny nor fully embrace, for it defied the iron-clad expectations of the life he had always known. The woman he loved seemed to radiate an unfiltered dignity, a purity that was untouched by the rigid constraints of society. She symbolised the freedom Arya had only ever dared to dream of — a space where he could simply be himself, stripped of the roles and responsibilities that weighed so heavily on him.

In her presence, Arya found himself unshackled. With her, there were no ancestral shadows casting doubt, no scrutinising eyes from an orthodox society that expected him to uphold the legacy of caste purity, tradition, and familial approval. She offered him something he had never experienced: an unbounded love that didn't demand compliance but rather invited authenticity. In her gaze, he saw the promise of a life lived openly, a life where the soul could roam free, untethered to obligations that felt like chains. For the first time, Arya was more than a dutiful son, a responsible elder sibling, a caretaker of his family's name. He was simply himself.

Yet, this realisation came with an undeniable weight. Arya knew his family would never accept her. His relatives and the society in which he had been raised would shun him, brand him an outcast, a renegade who had turned his back on everything they held sacred. She represented to them all that they despised, all that they feared — a rupture in the carefully woven fabric of respectability they had upheld for generations. She defied their lineage with her unconventional ways, her origins that bore no resemblance to the orthodox ideals his family revered.

The very thought of this rejection gnawed at Arya's heart. He could feel the silent disapproval that would ripple through his family if they knew. It would be a rejection not just of his choice but of his very essence, a dismissal so palpable that it would hurt more than any spoken condemnation. Their love had become a double-edged sword, its roots burrowing deeply, almost painfully, into the soil of his soul. It was love, yes, but love laced with sorrow, a love that would demand sacrifices he wasn't sure he could bear. But neither could he turn back nor he could carry forward; he was too deeply entangled with his own contemplation.

The decision had already bloomed in his heart, its roots entwining with the deepest parts of his spirit. It wasn't a decision he had consciously made but one that had emerged organically, quietly, as if his heart had known the path all along and had only been waiting for him to accept it. He had never before questioned the life laid out for him — a life built on respect, duty, and the silent acceptance of sacrifices for the greater good of his family. But now, he found himself rebelling against this unwritten code, his heart choosing a path that his mind would never dare to tread.

And then, there was the child. Her daughter, whose innocence reminded Arya of everything pure and untouched by the world's prejudices. In the child's eyes, Arya saw a fragile hope, a belief in a world that accepted people for who they truly were, not for where they came from or what names they bore. The girl looked up to him, a silent but eloquent trust reflected in her gaze, as if she believed in his ability to be both her guardian and her friend. In her, Arya found a new sense of responsibility — not just to the woman he loved but to this young soul who had unknowingly become a part of his life's new direction.

This bond with the child only strengthened his resolve, though it also deepened his inner conflict. He knew the road ahead would be fraught with hardship, that each step would bring him closer to a divide from his family that might never be bridged. Yet, with every passing moment, his heart leaned further toward this forbidden love, toward a life he had once thought impossible.

As days turned into weeks, weeks into years, Arya found himself at odds with his own identity. The man he had been — the dutiful son, the pillar of his family, the torchbearer of a long-standing legacy — was dissolving, making way for a man he barely recognised. He spent countless hours in introspection, questioning the path his heart was leading him down. Could he, a man raised to uphold the sanctity of tradition, truly defy it all for love?

Memories of his childhood surfaced during these moments of inner turmoil. He recalled the stories his father had told him, tales of ancestors who had sacrificed everything to uphold the family's honour. They were stories of valour and dignity, of unyielding adherence to principles that had guided their lineage through generations. To go against this was to challenge not just his family's values but the very foundation of his upbringing. The weight of his heritage bore down on him, a silent reminder of the expectations he was meant to fulfil.

Yet, love had a way of making even the most rational minds bend, of pushing the boundaries of what seemed impossible. The woman had become his sanctuary, a place where his soul found respite from the relentless expectations. When they were together, the walls he had built around himself seemed to crumble, and for a fleeting moment, he tasted the freedom he had never known he craved.

Arya knew that, in the eyes of his family, this was a betrayal. His love was a silent rebellion against everything they held dear. He imagined the conversations that would ensue, the disappointed gazes, the whispered condemnations. The thought of his parents' faces, etched with the pain of perceived failure, haunted him. They had invested their lives in raising him, in moulding him into a man who would carry forth their legacy. How could he face them now?

But then he would think of her, and all doubts would fade away. With her, he was not merely living – he was alive. She ignited within him a passion that transcended the mundanities of his existence, a desire not only for her but for a life that felt meaningful, real, and true to who he was. She was his muse, his catalyst for change, the one who made him question the very nature of duty and love.

As their love grew, so did the whispers within his family. Relatives began to notice his distant gaze, the way he would retreat into his thoughts, absent even when surrounded by his loved ones. His mother would cast worried glances in his direction, sensing that something had changed in her son, though she could not yet name it. His father, proud and stoic, maintained his silence, but Arya could feel the unspoken tension thickening each time he returned home.

In a society that valued conformity over individuality, Arya's rebellion was more than a personal choice; it was a statement. He was not merely challenging his family's expectations but the societal norms that had shaped him. Each step toward her was a step away from the identity he had spent his life cultivating. He was painfully aware that this path was a lonely one, marked by the heartbreak of those who loved him and the alienation that awaited him should he choose to follow his heart.

Yet, despite the risks, he could not bring himself to sever the connection. He had become too entwined with her, their lives interwoven in a way that felt ordained by something beyond his understanding. Love had awakened him, and there was no returning to the slumber of a life unexamined. He had tasted freedom, and even the thought of losing it was unbearable.

The bond he felt with her daughter further complicated his decision. He had grown attached to the child in ways he hadn't anticipated. Her innocence and belief in him had become an anchor in his storm-tossed heart, grounding him in the midst of his emotional chaos. She saw him not as a figure bound by tradition but as a person capable of love and warmth. In her presence, Arya felt a profound sense of purpose, as though he had been entrusted with a responsibility that went beyond the expectations of his family.

The night he made his final decision was a quiet one. Under a sky scattered with stars, Arya felt a calm resolve wash over him. He could no longer deny his heart's calling, that he was willing to endure the pain and sacrifice it demanded. He was prepared to face the consequences, to bear the weight of his family's disappointment, and to walk a path fraught with sorrow if it meant he could live a life that was truly his own.

As he stood there, gazing at the vast expanse above, he felt a sense of peace he hadn't known before. He was ready to step into the unknown, to embrace the life that awaited him, whatever it might bring. His heart had chosen, and he would follow its lead, come what may.

For Arya, this was not merely a choice between love and duty. It was a reclamation of his soul, a journey to find himself amidst the expectations that had defined him. He had come to understand that love was not a betrayal but a truth, a guiding light that would lead him, not away from his roots, but toward a deeper understanding of who he truly was.

Chapter III
The Silent Chains of Tradition and First Signs of Disapproval

As times passed by every raised eyebrow, every whispered remark, every silent judgment from his family etched a battle scar upon his heart. With every step he took towards her, he felt the weight of his family's expectations pressing upon him, their silent reproach a chain pulling him back into the world he once belonged to. He loved his family deeply; they were the people who had moulded him into the man he had become. The teachings and stories of his forefathers were woven into the very fabric of his being, and he cherished the legacy of wisdom passed down to him. This legacy surrounded him in everything he did. Even in the silence, he could hear the voices of his elders, urging him to remember his place, reminding him that his duty lay not in love but in loyalty to his lineage.

In his father, Arya saw the stern pride of their lineage, a man whose loyalty to tradition remained unwavering. Arya's father was not merely a figure in their household; he was a pillar, a respected presence that stood tall in their society, revered as the embodiment of Brahmin virtue. His wisdom was sought by the community. People would come to him for guidance, for help, for that pure, just, and untainted wisdom they believed only he could provide. To Arya, his father's words were truth itself, an immutable force that had guided him through life's uncertain paths like a beacon on a darkened shore.

But now, as Arya stood on the brink of a single choice, he found himself setting his own course, one that veered away from that guiding light. It was as if he were sailing into unknown waters, leaving the safety of his father's shore far behind. Arya's choice wasn't a simple decision; it was an affront, a quiet rebellion against everything their family represented. The very thought left him sleepless, his mind a storm of emotions that crashed and collided, tearing him between loyalty and self-discovery. He would lie awake at night, staring at the ceiling, feeling as if each tick of the clock was echoing the disappointment his father's presence cast over him—a wall he could not breach.

For Arya's father, his son's choice was not merely wrong; it was a betrayal, a rejection of the values and virtues he had spent a lifetime upholding. Each glance his father threw his way spoke louder than words. It was a silence filled with reproach, disappointment, and a sorrow Arya could almost touch. He felt it like a weight pressing down on him, one that seeped into his bones and made each step he took away from tradition feel like a burden he would carry forever.

And then, there was his mother. She had always been his shelter, his refuge from the world's judgments. She was wise, tender, and her love was a balm that Arya had come to depend upon since childhood. In her presence, he had always felt safe, a warmth that seemed unbreakable. Yet now, that same warmth was tinged with sorrow. Her eyes, usually so bright, were now tear-filled, and her voice trembled when she spoke to him, each word carrying both love and fear. She was watching him take a path that led away from everything she knew, and it pained her in ways Arya could feel with every glance.

Her silent suffering seemed to tear at him, a sorrow he knew he was causing. She had always guided him gently, her own values woven into her every word. But now, Arya could see her struggling to hold back, as if her heart was breaking for both her son and the traditions that had shaped their lives.

Arya's mind was a battlefield, torn between the man he wanted to become and the expectations that chained him to his past. Tradition was more than a set of rituals for his family; it was their identity, their anchor in the ever-shifting world. His father represented that anchor, unyielding and rooted in beliefs that stretched back through generations. But Arya felt a stirring within himself, an urge to question, to understand if there was more to life than the boundaries set by others. He wasn't rejecting his family's values out of spite; he simply wanted to explore what lay beyond them.

To him, the weight of tradition felt both comforting and suffocating. It was like a shadow that loomed over him, silent yet omnipresent, shaping his thoughts and actions even when he wished to step out of its grasp. His mind would often wander to the tales his father had told him as a child, stories of sages and ancestors who had walked the same path, never questioning, always abiding. They had lived lives that were pure, virtuous, and, in the eyes of his father, perfect. Arya's father expected the same from him, not just as a son, but as the next bearer of their family's legacy.

But Arya yearned to find his own voice amidst the echoes of the past. He wasn't asking to forsake his roots; he merely wanted the freedom to question, to understand, and perhaps, to grow in a direction that was his alone. Yet, each step he took in this direction felt like tearing at the very fabric that held his family together. In the eyes of his father, Arya's desire to carve his own path was not growth but betrayal.

The disapproval was unspoken yet palpable, filling the spaces of their home like a thick fog. At meals, his father's silence was deafening, his gaze a reminder of everything Arya was risking. His mother's face, once full of laughter, was now a mask of quiet sorrow. The house, which had once been a place of warmth, now felt like a shrine of expectations, each room echoing with the weight of unspoken judgments.

Arya would sometimes escape to the courtyard, where he could be alone with his thoughts under the open sky. He would look up at the stars and wonder if they, too, were bound by some ancient order or if they shone freely in the vastness. In those moments, he felt a kinship with the stars, each one a distant, flickering light fighting to be seen against the vast darkness. He wondered if he could find his own light, his own way of shining, without extinguishing the flame of his family's legacy.

Yet, even as he dreamed of freedom, Arya knew the path he was treading was filled with thorns. Each choice he made that took him further from his family's traditions was a wound, a small tear in the fabric of their bond. He feared that one day, those small tears would add up, and the bond would be severed completely. It was a fear that clung to him, one that kept him rooted even as he longed to soar.

In moments of doubt, Arya would replay his father's words in his mind, hoping to find some comfort in them. But the comfort was elusive, like trying to grasp water in his hands. His father's teachings were filled with wisdom, yet they felt distant, disconnected from the questions that haunted Arya's heart. The ideals of duty, honour, and sacrifice that his father upheld so fiercely were like an ancient script that Arya could not fully decipher.

He thought of his mother again, her tear-filled eyes, the silent plea in her gaze. She, too, was bound by tradition, yet her love was a force that transcended those chains. Arya knew that, no matter what path he chose, his mother's heart would ache for him, not because of the choices he made, but because she feared the pain that awaited him on this uncharted journey. Her love was like a fragile thread, stretched thin but unbroken, connecting them across the chasm that Arya felt growing between himself and his family.

In the end, Arya realised that the silent chains of tradition were not just imposed by his family; they were part of him, woven into his being. Breaking free was not as simple as walking away; it meant confronting the parts of himself that still clung to those values, questioning not just his family's beliefs but his own. He was both prisoner and guard, bound by chains he had yet to understand fully.

As he stood on this precipice, Arya felt the weight of generations pressing down on him. His choices would not just define his own life but echo through the legacy his family held dear. He was not blind to the pain he was causing, nor was he indifferent to the love and expectations that had shaped him. But he also knew that, without the courage to walk his own path, he would forever be haunted by the "what ifs" of a life half-lived.

In the quiet of the night, Arya whispered a silent promise to himself. He would value his family, not by following blindly, but by carrying their values in a way that resonated with his own truth. He would be the son they could be proud of, not because he conformed, but because he dared to question, to grow, and to build upon the foundation they had laid.

As the dawn broke, casting its golden light over the courtyard, Arya felt a sense of calm. He knew that the journey ahead would be fraught with challenges, misunderstandings, and perhaps even heartbreak. But he was ready to face it, carrying the silent chains of tradition not as a burden, but as a part of his identity, a reminder of where he came from, even as he set his sights on where he was going.

For Arya, this was the beginning of a new chapter, not just in his life but in the legacy of his family. He would be both keeper and creator, a bridge between the past and the future. And in that role, he found a strength he hadn't known he possessed—a strength born not of rebellion, but of love, respect, and the courage to be himself.

Chapter IV
War Within and The Reflection of Dharma

Arya's mind wandered to the teachings of the Bhagavad Gita that he had once read. The story of the Mahabharata had always felt distant, larger than life, a tale of gods, warriors, and moral dilemmas that seemed beyond the reach of ordinary existence. But now, the story felt close, intimate, as if it had been placed in his path to guide him through his own inner turmoil. He recalled Arjuna standing on the battlefield of Kurukshetra, torn between his duty as a warrior and his compassion for those he was meant to fight. Arya now understood that Kurukshetra was not merely a field of war; it was a symbol of the battle each soul must face within—a conflict between the roles and duties defined by society and the truth that lies within one's own heart.

In the great war of Kurukshetra, the most revered warrior Arjuna had stood against those who had shaped him—his family, his ideals, his teachers, and his guardians. He faced his uncles, his cousins, his elders, people who had been instrumental in his life. But when the moment came to choose between external loyalty and inner truth, he chose truth. Arya found himself in a similar position. Just as Arjuna had stood with his bow drawn, Arya now felt like, he was standing on his own Kurukshetra, his own battlefield. His war was not one of weapons or kingdoms, but of spirit and principles. It was a war not against his family's love but against the injustice that lay embedded within the rigidity of tradition. The battle he fought was not for land or power but for the freedom of his own soul—the right to honour a dignity that transcended caste, custom, and societal expectations.

Arya understood that unlike Arjuna, he would have to walk this path alone. There was no divine Krishna beside him, no charioteer to reveal the secrets of the universe. This journey was his own, and his truth was something he would have to uncover through his inner reflection and courage. His Dharma was not bound by the expectations others had of him but by the purity of his own convictions. His soul yearned to live a life that resonated with truth—a life that did not yield to the limitations of tradition but was free to honour love, equality, and compassion.

Dharma, Arya thought, was not about clinging to societal rules and customs; it was about understanding and embodying a universal truth that transcends these limitations. The world around him, with its myriad of customs and traditions, was but a tiny fragment of the universe's vast design. How could Dharma, the eternal law, be confined to the boundaries of human-made rules? Arya's thoughts spiralled into the depths of his inner universe, where he could feel the echoes of the divine calling him to a truth that went beyond superficial judgments.

Arya felt that he was part of something greater than his immediate community, greater even than the traditions that had defined his family for generations. The universe itself, in its endless expanse, held a truth that was beyond human understanding. Stars shone without discrimination, rivers flowed without prejudice, and the Earth embraced all beings equally. If nature itself did not impose divisions, how could his truth be bound by the narrow confines of caste and custom? His Dharma lay in following this universal law of compassion and equality, a law that did not differentiate but embraced all of creation in its boundless arms.

In this understanding, Arya felt an overwhelming sense of peace and liberation. He saw the truth as a flame burning steadily within him, a guiding light that was unaffected by the storms of external judgments. This inner flame represented love, wisdom, and the courage to stand by what he believed, even when it went against the norms and values he had been taught. Dharma, he understood, was not about following societal rules blindly but about accepting the deeper truth that resonated with the universe's own heartbeat.

Arya's family and society clung to customs that had been passed down through generations. These traditions were like ancient rivers, flowing through the lives of everyone around him, shaping them, confining them, and defining their destinies. Yet, Arya could see the illusion in these social constructs. He saw that while customs were meant to create harmony, they often did the opposite, breeding divisions and reinforcing hierarchies.

His heart yearned to break free from these illusions, to live a life that was aligned with the truth he felt within.

In his search for Dharma, Arya began to question the very foundation of societal norms. What was the purpose of a tradition that did not allow people to validate their true selves? How could customs that labelled love as wrong and discouraged the recognition of another's dignity be in alignment with the divine truth? The truth was much larger than any social construct; it was vast and boundless, encompassing the entire universe. Dharma was about recognising this larger truth, about embracing a reality that was beyond human-made divisions and prejudices.

Arya's inner universe was immense, an endless expanse where he felt connected to the cosmos. He knew that to truly align with Dharma, he had to rise above the judgments of society and revere the voice of truth within him. This truth was not something that could be dictated by others; it was a sacred knowing that resided in the depths of his soul. It called to him, urging him to live in harmony with the boundless existence that surrounded him.

As Arya delved deeper into his thoughts, he understood that the truth he sought was not an external authority but an inner realisation. It was a truth that could only be discovered within oneself, a truth that existed beyond words and concepts. He saw the universe as a mirror of his own consciousness, a reflection of the boundless truth that lay within him. To truly live by Dharma, he had to dignify this inner truth and accept it, regardless of the consequences.

Arya felt a profound sense of clarity. He understood that his journey was about embracing the truth within, even when it meant going against the norms of society. His family and community viewed Dharma as a set of rigid rules, a list of do's and don'ts that dictated one's actions. But Arya saw Dharma as a path of self-discovery, a journey toward understanding the true essence of existence. It was not about blindly following rules but about uncovering the divine truth that lay within his soul.

In this moment of clarity, Arya felt a connection to something far greater than himself. He saw the universe as a vast tapestry, woven with threads of love, compassion, and wisdom. His Dharma was to recognise this tapestry, to live in a way that reflected the truth he felt within. This truth was not limited by caste, customs, or social expectations; it was a universal truth that embraced all beings. This is one of the most profound realisations that Arya had been regarding love. Society had labelled his love as wrong, unworthy, simply because it did not fit within the framework of caste and social status. But Arya saw beyond these labels. He saw his beloved as a soul, a fellow traveller on the journey of life.

The love he felt was pure, untainted by societal judgments. It was a love that perceive the divine essence within the other, a love that was in perfect alignment with the truth of Dharma.

Arya understood that his Dharma was to honour and upheld this love, to cognize his beloved as his equal, not as someone defined by caste or status. His family saw her as a "lower" being, but Arya knew that this was a superficial label, a falsehood created by human minds. In his heart, he saw her as a reflection of the divine, a being of infinite worth and dignity. To deny this truth would be to betray his own soul.

He felt a sense of reverence for this love, a gratitude for the gift of connection that transcended worldly divisions. He knew that true love was not about possession or control; it was about accepting the other as a sacred being. His Dharma was to live in harmony with this truth, to stand by his beloved even when it meant going against the norms of society.

As Arya continued his journey of self-discovery, he began to see himself as part of a larger cosmic order. The universe was not merely an external reality but a reflection of his own inner consciousness. He was a part of this vast expanse, a drop in the ocean of existence. In recognising this, he felt a deep sense of humility and interconnectedness. His life was not separate from the stars, the rivers, or the trees; he was a part of the same universal consciousness that permeated all things.

This understanding gave him a sense of purpose. His Dharma was to live in alignment with this universal order, to respect the interconnectedness of all beings. The truth within him was the same truth that governed the cosmos—a truth of love, unity, and harmony. His journey was about finding this truth within himself and living it fully.

In this realisation, Arya found his true identity. He was not just a member of a particular family or caste; he was a soul, a spark of the divine, an expression of the universe itself. His life was a journey toward understanding and embodying this truth. He was not bound by the label's others had placed upon him; he was free to explore the depths of his own soul, to uncover the divine essence within.

Chapter V
Facing-off the Battlefield

As Arya prepared to step into the footsteps of family, a family he had, in past years, seen leave behind broken bonds and suspicions, he felt a heavy weight in his heart. His father was the embodiment of leadership within their revered Brahmin lineage, one that upheld the values of wisdom, knowledge, and spiritual guidance. Arya's father had aspired to uplift their people—a community long defined by intellectual and spiritual pursuits, confined by traditions and a rigid caste structure that didn't always allow for personal freedom. For Arya's father, Tradition and legacy was a sacred duty that shaped every aspect of his life and guided his role as a father, husband, and leader. But Arya saw more than just dharma in his father's life; he saw the sacrifices and personal losses that came with unwavering adherence to it.

Arya understood the expectations placed upon him—to be a model of wisdom, to uphold the virtues of his Brahmin heritage, to guide his community, and to respect the rules and practices that had been passed down for generations. But to Arya, fulfilling his duty also meant finding a partner who shared his ideals. He yearned for a woman who could be more than just a counterpart. She would need to be a soulmate, yes, but also a catalyst beyond that—a respected and admired master of her own personal dharma, someone who possessed her own strength and identity.

To Arya, this was not just about companionship; it was about finding someone who could help him weave a new legacy, one that valued tradition but was not bound by it. He dreamed of a relationship that would serve as a bridge between the old world and the new, carrying forward the values of their Brahmin lineage but with the freedom to question and reshape them in a way that aligned with the time.

Yet Arya was well aware that his father's ideals had cast a long shadow over the family, reaching out to every branch of their large extended clan. His father's influence stretched far and wide, shaping each member, binding them all to a path defined by dharma, even to the point that some family members could scarcely separate their own identities from it. His father was a revered figure, a man who had devoted his life to studying and embodying the sacred texts, performing rituals, and guiding others. Arya had grown up admiring this vision, yet a part of him felt the silent whisper of rebellion. His father's life was a tapestry of strong principles, yet in all those years, Arya noticed there was no personal, individual dharma that his father had embraced. Instead, he had adopted and internalised those shaped by generations past, traditions forged in a different era, for a different time.

As Arya grew older, he came to perceive that he could not solely follow the direction his father had once applied, always forcing himself to prioritise family unity over dharma, dignity, and equality. There was a fire within Arya that demanded something more—a desire for a life that integrate his values without the relentless weight of societal expectations. It was a journey filled with introspection, doubt, and moments of profound solitude. He often found himself questioning the purpose of duty, wondering if it could truly fulfil a man's life if it left his own spirit shackled. Arya had watched his father sacrifice personal joy in the name of duty, setting aside his own dreams for the family's sake. It was a sacrifice Arya both respected and resented. He knew that his father's choices had been made with love and a deep sense of obligation, yet he also knew that love could sometimes be blinding, hiding truths that lay just beneath the surface.

In the quiet of his room, Arya would often ponder these thoughts, feeling the weight of history on his shoulders. Somewhere within him, he felt a fierce independence, a defiant urge to carve his own path rather than follow one laid down by those who came before him. He knew he stood on stronger personal grounds because he never intended to take over or replace his father's role; he wanted to transcend it. He grew up as an observer, absorbing every teaching and every lesson from a distance, yet holding on to his unique perspective, refusing to be fully shaped by tradition.

Just as Arjuna faced his own loved ones on the battlefield of Kurukshetra, feeling his heart break at the thought of fighting his family and friends, Arya too felt his spirit tremble at the thought of opposing his own blood. The pain of standing against those he loved weighed heavily on him, often making him question the righteousness of his path. Arjuna had turned to Krishna, his divine charioteer, for guidance, seeking wisdom to understand his duty amidst such inner turmoil. For Arya, there was no Krishna to guide him. His battles were not fought with weapons, but with words, values, and beliefs that were just as piercing. In these moments of despair, it was his own consciousness that rose within him, speaking as a quiet but persistent voice of truth.

His conscience became his guiding force, reminding him of his purpose when the path grew dark, bolstering his spirit when he faltered. Just as Krishna had urged Arjuna to rise and perform his duty, Arya's inner voice whispered to him to stand firm, to embrace his destiny even if it meant confronting those he cherished. It was not a path devoid of love, but one that demanded strength, clarity, and the courage to uphold what he believed was right.

Every time he remembered the values his forefathers had instilled, Arya felt both a connection and a separation. The values of wisdom, compassion, self-discipline, and humility were deeply embedded in his heart. But he also knew that these values had come at a cost. The same sense of duty that bound his ancestors had also confined them, chaining them to a cycle of sacrifice and service that rarely allowed them the freedom to pursue their personal aspirations.

He saw his father's desire as a beloved elder's resolution, a powerful legacy handed down through the generations. Yet for Arya, it was a complicated inheritance, one that brought him both pride and pain. His father had once set Arya's heart apart, separating him in the hopes that he would one day follow in his footsteps. But Arya's heart held its own secrets, its own dreams, dreams that could not easily align with the life his father envisioned for him.

For Arya, life was a battlefield—a place where two worlds collided, where tradition met refinement, and where duty and desire wrestled for dominance. This internal conflict became the defining theme of his life, shaping his actions, his choices, and his relationships. In his mind, he saw himself standing at the edge of a vast field, a scholar and seeker preparing to face not an external enemy but the battles within his own soul. Each step he took was like a warrior advancing on the battlefield, feeling the weight of his ancestors, their hopes, their struggles, and their sacrifices.

He also saw love as a restrained tenderness that had always been his own seeking anchorage. Love, to him, was not merely a bond of hearts but a profound connection rooted in shared ideals, mutual respect, and an unwavering commitment to each other's growth. He had often imagined the type of woman he would want by his side—someone who would stand as his equal, who would bring balance to his spirit and strengthen his resolve. In his mind's eye, she was more than a partner; she was a mirror to his soul, reflecting both his strengths and weaknesses, encouraging him to be the best version of himself.

The ideal partner for Arya was more than a reflection of his dreams; she was his counterpart in every way. Whenever he allowed himself to dream of her, he could see her strength, her wisdom, her disappointment, and her hope. He could see the world of her own soul, a world that resonated deeply with his own, yet one that existed independently of his desires. Arya knew that a woman like her would need to be fiercely independent, grounded in her own sense of purpose, not afraid to challenge him and push him beyond his comfort zone. This vision of a soulmate, while beautiful, was not without its own challenges. Arya understood that finding such a person would mean facing his own fears, letting go of his need for control, and opening himself up to the vulnerability that true love demands.

In the depths of his soul, Arya felt the weight of his ancestors. The teachings of his father were like the mantras etched into his heart, ready to guide him on this battlefield of life. But his own heart, with its yearning for love and fulfilment, could not always align with the path set before him. The lineage that Arya belonged to was revered and unshakeable, a lineage that placed wisdom, selflessness, and devotion to dharma above all else. His forefathers had faced challenges that Arya could only imagine, standing against the tide of worldly distractions, renouncing desires for the greater good, and dedicating themselves to the pursuit of knowledge and spiritual growth.

And yet, here was Arya, standing on the threshold of a new era, torn between upholding his lineage and exploring his own dreams. His mind raced as he grappled with the weight of tradition, the expectations of his family, and the calling of his own heart. He knew that his journey would not be easy, that he would face resistance from those who believed that duty to family and tradition should come before personal happiness.

Chapter VI
Crossing the Threshold

Arya moved forward, feeling the disapproval of his family and the cold judgment of his relatives. The entire world seemed to press its weight upon him, society's eyes fixed on him with abandonment. Yet, as he moved closer to the woman he loved, in her eyes he saw no shame, no fear—only trust and love.

That day, Arya chose to confront his family, ascending the stairs of his home with a heart filled with dread and determination. His father's gaze met him like a wall of stone, his mother's sorrow resonating like a silent lament. His siblings looked upon him with disappointment, casting him as the betrayer of their shared heritage. But Arya's heart was resolute. He had already crossed the threshold within himself; he could not turn back. Taking the hand of that woman and her child felt like crossing a bridge from which he could never return. It was a simple gesture, yet it symbolised everything, signalling his decision to all who watched.

He felt as though he had crossed a bridge, leaving behind the man his family had expected him to be. But he found his dharma, his purpose, his truth. He knew that his choice was his own, and it was unshakable. The love he held for her, the belief in dignity was his path now. He would be his own guide, upholding a dharma that resonated not with lineage, but with the depths of his spirit.

And yet, as the days wore on, doubt began to creep back into his heart. Arya found himself haunted by the echoes of his family's disappointment, their looks of betrayal, and the silent heaviness of his mother's sorrow. Each memory was a whisper, a question that lingered in his mind— "Have I done the right thing?" The weight of these questions bore down on him like the relentless waves of an unseen ocean, threatening to erode the foundation of his conviction.

During quiet moments, Arya thought of Arjuna on the battlefield of Kurukshetra, standing amidst his family, his kin, his beloved teachers, and friends. He remembered Arjuna's heart shattering as he saw those, he loved standing as his enemies, the anguish that had driven him to the edge of despair. In those moments, Arya felt an affinity with Arjuna's inner turmoil, his reluctance to raise a weapon against those he cherished. Arya, too, had felt that same turmoil, that same breaking of the heart, as he took his stand against his own family's expectations and traditions.

But while Arjuna had the divine guidance of Krishna, Arya had only his own conscience to guide him through the darkness. There was no charioteer by his side, no voice to remind him of his duty and his purpose. He was left to wrestle with his doubts alone, to face the battlefield within his own heart.

In those moments of solitude, Arya's faith in his choice wavered, clouded by fears of abandonment and failure. He questioned if he was strong enough to carry this burden alone, if he could withstand the isolation and the judgment. He knew his family and society expected him to return, to admit that his decision was a mistake, to restore the balance that he had disrupted.

Yet, something within him—call it his conscience, his inner voice—whispered that turning back would mean erasing the path he had chosen, denying his own truth. He understood that the life he had left behind was comfortable, but it was not his own. To go back would mean surrendering the authenticity he had fought so hard to claim.

One night, Arya sat beneath the stars, letting the vast silence of the universe wash over him. He closed his eyes, inhaling deeply, and allowed himself to feel the full weight of his choice. The starlit sky seemed to mirror his own inner expanse—a wide, open void filled with both beauty and terror, freedom and uncertainty.

He asked himself the questions that had plagued him, that had remained unanswered. What was he truly afraid of? Was it the judgment of others, or was it the fear of standing alone? Was it the pain of separation, or was it the possibility that he might not be enough, that he might fail in his pursuit of a life carved from his own truth?

Slowly, he began to understand that his fears were not something to be vanquished. They were, in fact, parts of himself that needed acknowledgment. They were reminders of his humanity, the depth of his love for his family, and the loyalty ingrained within him. He came to realise that courage was not the absence of fear, but the decision to keep moving forward in spite of it.

In this understanding, Arya felt a quiet strength settle within him. He saw that his journey was not a denial of his heritage but an evolution of it. By forging his own path, he was honouring his family's legacy in a way that resonated with his own soul, even if it defied their expectations. His true duty was to the truth within himself, a truth that would allow him to live in harmony with his own spirit, even if the world around him could not understand.

The following days saw Arya wrestling with his inner conflict, confronting the lingering shadows of guilt and regret. Each time he felt the pull of doubt, he reminded himself that he had crossed a threshold that could not be undone. His decision was his own, and he would stand by it, no matter the cost.

One evening, as he sat beside the woman he loved, he felt a sense of peace in her presence. She was his partner in this journey, a quiet strength that grounded him. Together, they were building a life that was honest and true, a life that did not depend on the approval of others but was guided by mutual respect and love. He understood that this was his new family, his chosen path, and he found solace.

And yet, he also knew that his journey was far from over. He would continue to face moments of doubt, times when the burden of his decision would feel too heavy to bear. But he had found within himself a reservoir of strength, a faith in his own ability to withstand whatever trials lay ahead. He was no longer a prisoner of others' expectations; he was a man who had claimed his own life, who had crossed the threshold into a future of his own making.

Under the starlit sky, Arya lay down, feeling the earth beneath him, steady and unyielding. He was reminded of the lesson Arjuna had learned on the battlefield—that true dharma lies not in adherence to tradition, but in alignment with one's own heart and soul. Arya's journey had brought him to that same understanding, and with it, a sense of peace.

He closed his eyes, letting the stillness of the night envelop him. His heart was no longer burdened by fear or regret. He had crossed the threshold, and while he did not know what lay beyond, he was ready to face it, armed with the quiet courage of a man who had found his own truth.

Chapter VII
The True Victory

Arya moved forward, each step feeling as though he were wading through an invisible current of resistance. The disapproval of his family and the cold judgment of his relatives hung over him like a thick mist, clouding his vision and weighing down his spirit. It was as if the entire world had conspired to bind him to a life that wasn't his own. Society's eyes, unblinking and unyielding, fixed upon him with the quiet rage of abandonment.

Yet Arya's heart was resolute, fortified by a decision that had been born from long, painful nights of solitude and soul-searching. He had already crossed the threshold within himself; there was no turning back. Taking her hand in his, he felt the profound symbolism of that simple gesture, as though he were stepping onto a bridge that would burn behind him. He was crossing over from the world he had known into a realm of his own choosing, and there would be no return.

In that singular moment, he had defied his lineage, the moral that had bound him, and the unspoken weight of his society's expectations. He felt as though he had crossed an unseen boundary, leaving behind the man his family had crafted from their dreams and traditions. But he had discovered something far more precious—his dharma, his purpose, his truth. He knew now that his choice was his own, and no force on earth could shake it. The love he held for her and the integrity that now defined him were his path, a path only he could walk.

And yet, as the days passed, the shadows of doubt crept into Arya's heart, curling around his resolve like mist. He was haunted by echoes of his family's sorrow, the disappointment carved into their faces, and the silent, heart-breaking weight of his mother's grief. Each memory was a question, a wound that refused to heal, whispering relentlessly in the quiet of his mind—Have I done the right thing?

As he found himself struggling, entangled in these questions, bearing their weight as though they were chains binding him to a past, he could not entirely forsake. He remembered Arjuna on the battlefield of Kurukshetra, standing amidst kin and blood, paralysed by the understanding that he must fight those he loved. Arya understood now, in a way he had never before, the depth of Arjuna's agony as he had faced his beloved teachers, friends, and family standing on the opposite side.

Like Arjuna, Arya's heart shattered at the thought of severing himself from the people who had shaped his identity, his sense of belonging. He felt the same urge to abandon his duty, to let the overwhelming grief and guilt consume him. But while Arjuna had been blessed with the divine guidance of Krishna, who reminded him of his purpose, Arya was alone. There was no celestial charioteer by his side, no godly voice to cut through the fog of his despair. He had only his own conscience, faint but resilient, to guide him.

Every judgmental glance, every whispered insult he encountered felt like a dagger, a reminder of the cost of his decision. Society did not easily forgive those who chose to carve their own path, nor did it show mercy to those who disrupted the ancient fabric of tradition. He was, to them, a heretic, a soul lost to the temptations of rebellion, and they cast him out accordingly. In his darkest hours, Arya replayed his father's scorn, his mother's grief, and his siblings' resentment. He saw in them a pain as vivid as his own, the fractured dreams and broken expectations that he had left in his wake. In these moments, he wondered if he could endure the loneliness that now stretched before him—a path shrouded in shadows, unlit by the familiar glow of family or community. He questioned whether he had the strength to carry on without the comfort of his family's love.

But in the depths of his despair, a quiet voice within him began to rise, like the first rays of dawn breaking over the horizon. This voice, steady and patient, reminded him of why he had chosen this path. It whispered to him of freedom, of the unbreakable bond he had formed with his own soul. It spoke of a journey that was not about rejection, but about transformation—a journey that allowed him to uphold his heritage by seeking his truth, not by obeying out of fear.

He began to see that his inner struggles, his doubts, were not signs of weakness but of growth. He understood that courage was not the absence of fear, but the ability to move forward despite it. He did not need to be invincible; he only needed to be steadfast.

One evening, Arya sat alone beneath the stars, the vastness of the universe pressing down upon him, filling him with both awe and humility. He allowed himself to feel the full weight of his emotions—fear, grief, guilt, and a longing for the life he had left behind. He surrendered to these feelings, letting them flow through him like a river, neither resisting nor denying them. And in that surrender, he found a profound peace, a stillness that settled into his bones.

In that stillness, he recalled Arjuna's lesson—that true dharma was not about conforming to the world's expectations, but about aligning one's actions with the truth of one's own soul. Arya understood that his duty was not to follow the dictates of his family or society, but to recognise and respect the voice within him that spoke of love, courage, and authenticity. His dharma lay in being true to himself, in upholding a path that resonated not with the lineage of his blood, but with the lineage of his spirit.

As he stood beneath the stars, breathing in the cool night air, Arya felt his resolve crystallise, becoming as clear and unbreakable as the night sky above. He knew now that he would walk this path not because it was easy, but because it was right. He had crossed the threshold, and in doing so, he had stepped into the fullness of his own being.

In the days that followed, Arya's understanding deepened. He came to see that his defiance was not a rejection of his family's values, but an affirmation of their essence. The strength and resilience he had inherited were not chains binding him to a single path, but wings that allowed him to soar into the unknown. He had become the living embodiment of their legacy—not in conformity, but in the courage to forge his own way.

To society, he was a man who had forsaken his heritage, an outcast. But Arya no longer sought validation from the world outside; he had found a source of strength within himself, an unshakeable foundation rooted in his own truth. Arya's journey was not one of choosing between family and self, but of expanding his heart to hold both the love for his heritage and the freedom to define it in his own terms.

Beside him, the woman he had chosen stood as his equal, his partner in this daring journey. She was not merely his love, but his mirror, reflecting back to him the courage and grace he often doubted within himself. In her presence, he felt whole—a man who had traversed the abyss of fear and emerged, scarred but unbroken, on the other side.

And though he knew that the road ahead would be fraught with challenges, Arya felt a newfound lightness, a sense of liberation. The expectations that had once burdened him now seemed like distant echoes, reminders of a past that no longer defined him. He was no longer bound by the silent commands of society or the weight of ancestral duty. He had transcended them, not in defiance but in the quiet dignity of self-discovery.

As he stood beneath the vast, indifferent sky, Arya breathed deeply, feeling his spirit expand, unencumbered and unafraid. He knew that he had only begun this journey, that there were many battles yet to be fought, doubts yet to be faced. But he was no longer alone. He had crossed the threshold, not only into a new life, but into a new understanding of himself—a man who had found his truth and was ready to live it.

And in that moment, Arya discovered that he was free—not because he had abandoned his past, but because he had finally claimed it as his own.

www.ingramcontent.com/pod-product-compliance
Lightning Source LLC
LaVergne TN
LVHW041633070526
838199LV00052B/3344